Kids love reading
Choose Your Own Adventure®!

"These books are like games. Sometimes the choice seems like it will solve everything, but you wonder if it's a trap."

Matt Harmon, age 11

"I think you'd call this a book for active readers, and I am definitely an active reader!"

Ava Kendrick, age 11

"You decide your own fate, but your fate is still a surprise."

Chun Tao Lin, age 10

"Come on in this book if you're crazy enough! One wrong move and you're a goner!"

Ben Curley, age 9

"You can read *Choose Your Own Adventure* books so many wonderful ways. You could go find your dog, or follow a unicorn."

Celia

TROUBLE ON PLANET EARTH

BY R. A. MONTGOMERY

ILLUSTRATED BY
MARIANO TROD, CLAUDIO GRIGLIO, AND ANDRÉS ROSSI
COVER BY MARCO CANNELLA

CHOOSECO
WAITSFIELD, VERMONT

Book design: Stacey Boyd, Big Eyedea Visual Design

For information regarding permission, write to:

CHOOSECO®

P.O. Box 46
Waitsfield, Vermont 05673
www.cyoa.com

Publisher's Cataloging-In-Publication Data

Names: Montgomery, R. A. | Trod, Mariano, illustrator. |
  Griglio, Claudio, illustrator. | Rossi, Andrés, illustrator.
  | Cannella, Marco, illustrator.
Title: Trouble on planet Earth / by R.A. Montgomery ;
  illustrated by Mariano Trod, Claudio Griglio, and Andrés
  Rossi ; cover by Marco Cannella.
Other Titles: Choose your own adventure ; 11.
Description: [Revised edition]. | Waitsfield, Vermont :
  Chooseco, [2006] | Originally published: Toronto ; New York
  : Bantam Books, ©1984. | Summary: Earth's oil reserves have
  gone missing overnight. When the trail takes you to outer
  space, you find that a mysterious galaxy beyond the Milky
  Way seems to be siphoning Earth's oil using laser straws. By
  choosing specific pages, you determine the outcome.
Identifiers: ISBN 1-933390-11-5 | ISBN 978-1-933390-11-6
Subjects: LCSH: Petroleum reserves—Juvenile fiction. |
  Interplanetary voyages—Juvenile fiction. | CYAC: Petroleum
  reserves—Fiction. | Interplanetary voyages—Fiction. | LCGFT:
  Science fiction. | Choose-your-own stories. | Action and
  adventure fiction.
Classification: LCC PZ7.M7684 Tr 2006 | DDC [Fic]—dc23

Published simultaneously in the United States and Canada

Printed in Malaysia

20 19 18 17 16 15 14 13 12 11

For Anson and Ramsey

And
For Avery and Lila

And for Shannon

BEWARE and WARNING!

This book is different from other books.

You and YOU ALONE are in charge of what happens in this story.

There are dangers, choices, adventures, and consequences. YOU must use all of your numerous talents and much of your enormous intelligence. The wrong decision could end in disaster—even death. But don't despair. At any time, YOU can go back and make another choice, alter the path of your story, and change its result.

The Earth's oil fields are drying up and the world is thrown into chaos. As you watch the news reports, your brother Ned has one of his premonitions: the Earth's oil is being stolen. But who would steal it? And how? Should you put your investigation skills to work in Saudi Arabia, another of Ned's "premonitions"? Or should you travel first to CIA Headquarters to see what they have to say?

Let's hope the Earth's fuel lasts long enough to let you find out!

1

"Good evening. Tonight we bring you a special report from our news team on the mounting crisis. Interviews with leaders around the world, from Paris, Cairo, Beijing, Moscow, and Washington, confirm that no answer has been found to the sudden loss of oil in every oil field in the world."

You turn from the evening news and jab your brother in the ribs.

"Hey, Ned, this is it! It's finally happening. There's no more oil. The Earth is giving up."

"Maybe the oil is being stolen. Maybe there's some international plot to drive up prices."

Ned is famous for his crazy ideas, and you and he have gained an international reputation for solving problems no one else can tackle. You're especially good at analyzing data and developing solutions, but Ned goes on instinct and ESP.

Together you're an excellent team. The trouble with Ned is you have to keep reminding him that it's a team. He's always out for his own glory.

"Stolen? Come on, Ned. Who could steal it? It's just been used up. There isn't enough oil anyway, at least not the way we're using it."

Turn to the next page.

2

Ned stares at you, and that look comes over his face. It's a look you know only too well, the look he gets when the special knowledge hits him— knowledge from some secret source. Even Ned can't explain it. It just happens to him.

"I feel the knowledge," he announces. "It's up to us. We'll crack this case."

"Now I suppose you want us to find out who's taking the oil and bring it back. Right? Am I right?"

He nods, adjusts his glasses, and reaches for the world atlas on the desk.

On your last investigation, you and Ned solved the strange phenomenon of the melting statues in the National Museum. Before that came the case of the missing airliner, and before that your most grisly case: the trunk murders in Arizona.

Ned looks up from the atlas. His index finger rests on the map of the Middle East.

"I say we begin the search right here in Saudi Arabia. That's where the oil loss was first discovered, according to the news."

"No, Ned, I say we start by going to Washington, D.C. and offering our help to the government. The CIA."

"Let's flip a coin," Ned answers.

"Okay. Heads or tails?"

If you choose heads, turn to page 3.

If you choose tails, turn to page 4.

The coin comes up heads, and you win. You and Ned head for Washington. You don't expect much trouble getting to the CIA. Your help in finding the missing Boeing 747 established your reputation there. You and Ned discovered an abandoned airfield in the Andes where the plane was taken after it was hijacked by a terrorist band. Ned got the secret information—by intuition, ESP, whatever—but, as usual, it came in a strange language that you alone understand.

Turn to page 9.

The coin comes up heads—so you lose. "Okay, Ned. You always win! It's that lucky intuition you've got. Lead the way. On to Saudi Arabia."

You start packing the emergency kit you always bring along on your adventures.

"Hey, Ned, what did you do with the automatic direction finders?"

"They're in the top drawer of the bureau," he answers. "Hurry up, will you?"

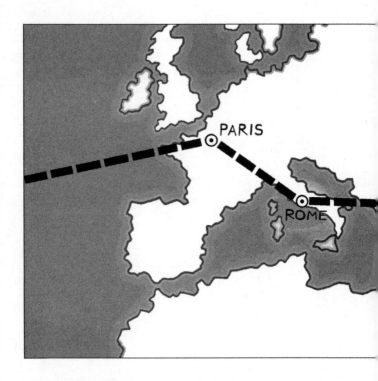

Finally you're packed and off to the airport. Thanks to the rewards you earned on your earlier cases, you have plenty of cash for the trip.

Your plane makes stops in Paris and Rome and finally arrives in Riyadh, Saudi Arabia's crowded, hot capital city. Once off the plane, you blink in the white heat of full day and wonder what your next step is.

"You got us here, Ned—the oil capital of the world. What now?" you ask.

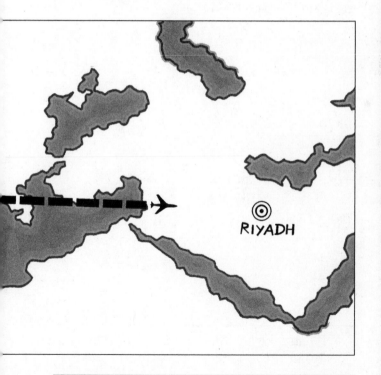

RIYADH

Turn to the next page.

6

Ned stands rigid in the milling crowd outside the airport and begins to pivot slowly, a human compass preparing to lead the way. But before he stops, a small, fat man with eyeglasses perched on a nose like a falcon's, interrupts.

"Pardon, most honored guests of our humble land," he says. "You are tourists needing a hotel, rest from the trip, and a tour of the city. Am I not right? I know I am right. You must avail yourselves of the services of Bahib Mefiz, one of the finest guides in this barren land."

If you take his offer and head for a hotel to rest after the long plane ride, turn to page 13.

If you reject his offer, turn to page 18.

Once you arrive at the Central Intelligence Agency just outside Washington, D.C., you are cordially ushered into the director's private office. Martha Thornberry sits behind a large steel desk and smiles at you both.

"Welcome! I hoped you'd come. We certainly can use your help. As usual, Special Section hasn't a clue as to what's going on. Remember, though, this is our secret. If Congress ever found out we were using a couple of kids, they'd close us up tighter than a microwave oven."

"Okay, we promise. What now?" you ask.

Turn to the next page.

Ms. Thornberry stares into space for a second. Then she speaks.

"This is the way I see it. There are two possible solutions. We've heard rumors hinting at a master plan for world domination that is based on energy control. The group supposedly behind it is called OWD, Organization for World Domination. Of course they use that name among themselves, not publicly. We suspect a front group called Organization for World Prosperity is their public face."

She opens the one dossier on her desk.

"But frankly at this point we have no idea who's behind it, if anyone, or what's causing it. A famous nuclear scientist we've been in contact with thinks a nuclear accident is what's making the oil disappear."

If you decide to investigate OWD first, go on to the next page.

If you decide to contact the nuclear scientist, turn to page 12.

"Let's start with the OWD plot, Ms. Thornberry," you say.

Ms. Thornberry nods and opens her desk, pulling out a manila envelope marked TOP SECRET. She breaks the thick red seal. From the envelope she removes a map, three sheets of paper covered with equations and figures, and a set of photographs.

"Here, look at this," she says. "This is about all we've got on OWD. It's a shadowy group—part fanatics committed to some political leader who died years ago, part terrorists who love trouble for its own sake. Worst of all, we think OWD is controlled by a wealthy man named Hugo. This Hugo is reported to be crazy but shrewd. He'll be a formidable adversary."

"That's all the name you've got, Hugo? No full name?" you ask.

"I'm afraid that's it. We assume, of course, that it's not his real name."

One of the papers is a world map with the locations of all known oil fields. Next to each oil field is a figure for the number of barrels produced per day and the final destination of the oil.

"Wait!" you exclaim. "Look at this!"

Turn to page 14.

Ned nods his head several times. "Nukes are no good. Should have known it all along," he mutters.

"What do you mean, Ned? What should you have known?"

He ignores you and turns to Ms. Thornberry.

You whisper to yourself, "Just one more time Neddie—one more time ignoring me and you'll find out about the nuclear bomb in my fist, you beanbrain."

"What's that you said?" he asks.

You've had to put up with "Ned the Genius" all your life. It's always been the same. "Boy wizard solves mystery." You are mentioned in the articles as the translator, but he gets the credit. What's more, he's only a year older than you. That really hurts. Even worse is the real truth—that you actually solve most of the mysteries. Ned gets good leads but it's left up to you to figure things out. Just once you'd like to show him up. You deserve to be the hero.

"Enough bickering, you two," Ms. Thornberry cuts in. "I don't have time for that. Here's the folder on Dr. Helmut Saragura. He's the one who thinks the oil drain is linked to a nuclear accident." She holds out the folder and you grab it before Ned can make a move.

"Not *the* Helmut Saragura?" you ask.

"Who else?"

Turn to page 17.

"Fine. Take us to a hotel," you say. "We're exhausted."

"At your service. Please to get into my most humble taxi," answers Bahib Mefiz, rubbing his hands in satisfaction.

When you arrive at the hotel, you are ushered to your rooms, and you quickly fall asleep. Hours later, mildly refreshed, you and Ned are seated in your room, studying a piece of paper that was slipped under Ned's door while he was sleeping. It bears the following inscription:

ZOCKUS, ZORCUS, HARUM COOR
LEDURN RODURN
MORDA FEWER

Ned stares at the inscription, whispering it over and over again.

There is a sudden knock at the door. When you open it, there stands Bahib Mefiz, smiling and twisting his key ring in his moist hands.

"Now is the time, my friends, the time to go," he announces.

Ned turns, his face ashen. He has the frozen look he bears only when the special knowledge hits him.

You run to his side. "What is it, Ned?"

"It's too late," he murmurs. "Too late."

Turn to page 20.

14

"Look at these dates!"

You point to the numbers next to each oil center marked on the map. One date is the beginning of the great oil drain, three weeks back—the very day the Saudis first began noticing the problem in their fields.

"Where did you get these papers, Ms. Thornberry?" you ask.

"I shouldn't divulge our sources, but they came from a man named Boris, a highly placed member of the OWD group. He came over to our side several years ago."

Ned turns pale. His eyelids begin to flutter strangely, his head turns around, and he speaks:

"Narimbo! Narimbo! Ita Maguro."

Before Ms. Thornberry can ask you what it means, you blurt out the translation.

"It means that we don't have much time. Boris is asking us to act now. He says get to the oil fields in Egypt right away."

Ned's special information is usually right, but your native caution is making you wonder if you shouldn't try to contact Boris before rushing off to the oil fields. The OWD group plays for keeps, according to Ms. Thornberry. Murder is an everyday event for them. And they hate snoops.

If you go straight to the oil fields in Egypt, turn to page 23.

If you decide to contact Boris first, turn to page 25.

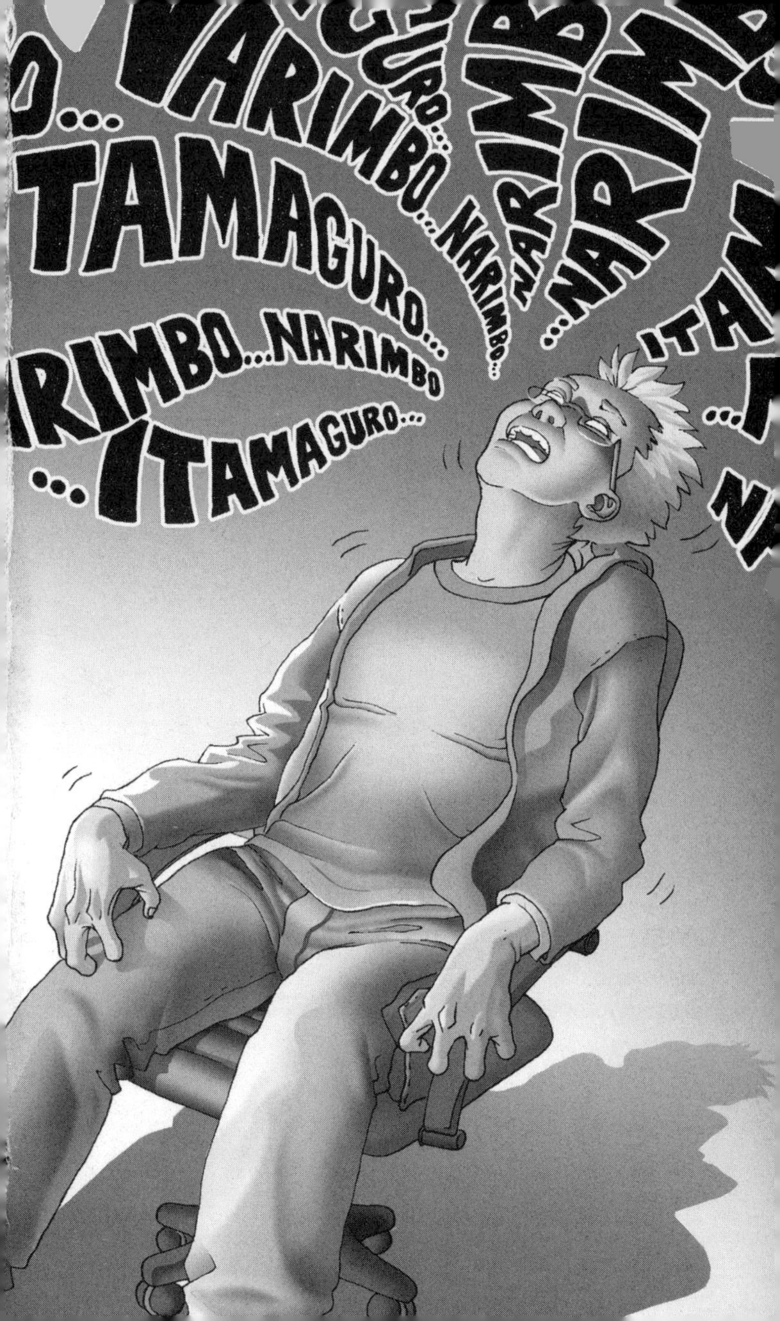
ITAMAGURO...
RIMBO...NARIMBO
...ITAMAGURO...
GURO...
ARIMBO...NARIMBO...
NARIMBO...
...NARI
ITA

Helmut Saragura is world-famous. Though most of his fellow scientists think he's a crank, all of them concede that he's a genius. You've always dreamed of meeting him.

His folder outlines two possible solutions to the problem. First, Saragura suggests that the disappearance of the oil could be linked to the disposal of the world's nuclear waste. Second, he mentions ominous, partially verified rumors of a massive core meltdown at a nuclear plant on a remote island in the South Pacific—a volcanic island shrouded in a perpetual mist and belonging to no country.

You don't know how the island, or even the nuclear waste, could be linked to the oil problem, but Helmut Saragura is a very brilliant scientist. You might as well follow up on one of his suggestions.

If you choose to explore the nuclear waste problem first, turn to page 41.

If you decide to head for the mysterious island, turn to page 40.

18

"No, we don't really need your services," you say. "Thanks anyway."

The man bows low, murmurs his regrets, and disappears into the crowd.

"Ned, wait a minute, will you? I want to get a newspaper at the foreign magazine stand. We'd better keep up with what's happening. I'll be right back."

Ned nods, and you duck back into the air-conditioned calm of the airport. Minutes later, you emerge with the latest edition of the overseas English-language *Herald Tribune*.

Ned is nowhere to be seen!

You search for him, calling his name. There's no answer.

"Where is he now? Leave it to him to get lost. He's up to his old tricks," you say to yourself crossly.

At that moment an old man taps you lightly on the arm and speaks in heavily accented English.

"Your brother awaits you. Have no fear. Allah be praised!"

Turn to page 22.

"Okay, Ned, I'll check in at the hotel," you say. But there's no answer. Ned is too absorbed in the mandalas.

At the hotel you get adjoining rooms. Then you settle down to wait for Ned on your terrace, sipping iced mint tea. Hours pass in the dull heat of this arid land. Still no Ned. By six o'clock you're panicky. Ned does have a habit of forgetting where he is, but you're sure that something is very wrong this time.

You go back to the mandala shop, but the shopkeeper says Ned left hours ago. You go to the local police, but they don't seem to be interested.

"Many people disappear here for a few days. There are many sights. He'll be back," says a bored police officer sitting behind a battered desk.

At the United States Embassy, a young duty officer takes Ned's name and description, notes the last place he was seen, and yawns. "Well, time will tell," he says.

"No, it won't! We don't have time! Get my brother back right now! We're American citizens, you know!"

Turn to page 31.

"Too late for what, Ned?" you ask urgently.

Bahib snaps his fingers and Ned comes out of his trance.

"Allow me to introduce myself. I am not really Bahib Mefiz. I am Gaston Patty, Director of Secret Projects for Interpol, the finest group of police officers in the world, united beyond national barriers in our fight against crime and corruption."

He makes a small bow. You certainly know about Interpol, but this is a surprise.

"I know of you people," he continues. "Your movements are watched by our agents. Your reputation as amateur detectives is well-respected. When you headed for here, I simply intercepted you. And now, let us continue on to the missing oil."

"Too late! It's too late. It's all gone," says Ned in a distant, hazy voice. You can see that he has not completely recovered.

"Come on now, Ned. How do you know? Is that what the message on the paper says?" you ask him.

Ned shakes his head. "I don't really know. I just feel it."

Go on to the next page.

Gaston Patty steps across to examine the strange message. Then he turns to both of you.

"If Ned thinks there is a message of importance in this strange incantation, then I suggest we take it to a famous astrologer. He may be able to unlock the secret if you two can't."

Moments later, the three of you are in the crowded streets of Riyadh on the way to the astrologer. The swarming crowd makes it hard to see where you're going. For just a moment you bend down to tie your shoe, and when you straighten up, Ned and Monsieur Patty are gone.

Turn to page 54.

22

You stare at the old man for several moments before speaking. He does not move. "How did you know about my brother, anyway?" you ask him.

The old man smiles and says, "Oh, it is simple. I observed you two. It is my business to watch. You will find him in that shop over there. The one with the paintings."

He melts into the crowd and disappears.

Sure enough, Ned is just where the old man said he was. The tiny shop sells intricate geometric paintings called mandalas. They're used by Muslims to stimulate mystical trances. Ned is absorbed in looking at one mandala painting.

"Come on, Ned, we've got work to do."

"You go ahead. These mandalas are fabulous. I'll catch up, don't worry. Check in at the main hotel, the Mara. I'll be along."

What now?

*If you leave Ned and go to the hotel,
turn to page 19.*

If you wait for him, turn to page 32.

"We'll go straight to Egypt," you answer. "Can you get us there?"

Ms. Thornberry uses the red phone on her desk, which connects her directly to the Oval Office.

"Yes, Mr. President. That's right. Of course. You have my assurance. No. Congress will never know."

She hangs up and turns to you, smiling.

"Okay. It's all arranged. The President has approved a special flight of the latest Z40 global reconnaissance plane to take you to Cairo, Egypt. You'll be there before you know it."

Turn to page 29.

"Ms. Thornberry, we have to talk to Boris. The message Ned is getting will lead him to Boris. You shouldn't throw him off the track," you say.

Ms. Thornberry paces around the room. She stops, stares out at the CIA grounds below, and ponders for a second.

"Okay, I'll arrange it. But you've got to take Tony Ditwiller with you. He is one of our best agents."

"Not Ditwiller again! He was with us in the Andes. The guy is a pain."

Ms. Thornberry stares at you, speaking in a soft voice that always spells trouble.

"Ditwiller is a professional who does what he has to. Nothing more, nothing less. He will go with you to Morocco. That's where Boris was last seen. Good luck."

You decide to try to lose Ditwiller as soon as possible.

Turn to page 39.

The coast is clear. You creep up the stairs. Once again good luck shines on you: the door is unlocked. Slowly you push it open and enter, careful not to make a sound.

Unbelievable! The room is now filled with the blinking lights of a huge computer. It must have been covered by a screen when you were in the room the first time.

Huddled over the computer keyboard is a person about your height. He is so busy he doesn't even hear you enter.

On the display screen above the keyboard is what looks to you like an intricate maze.

"Eureka! I've got it!" shouts the person at the computer. With that he turns and sees you for the first time.

You stifle a scream. The person has no face at all! Where his eyes, nose, and mouth should be, there are a television screen and a speaker instead.

And before your eyes the creature begins to change form. It shrinks in size until it is a glowing red mass about the size of a pumpkin.

Turn to page 30.

Within 24 hours, you and Ned find yourselves in Egypt riding in a small truck, bumping along a dusty road past a group of pyramids. Ned gives your driver directions, which come straight from his unknown source. This "source" can be very annoying. It makes Ned act like a know-it-all, and sometimes he's wrong!

"Look, look at that, Ned." You point to the smallest pyramid. Sunlight is flashing off a reflecting surface near its peak.

Ned stares, then shrugs his shoulders.

"It's nothing."

"Ned, look! It's flashing some kind of message. In code. Three short flashes—pause—three long, three short. Come on, Ned."

"It's nothing. We have to get to the oil fields."

If you trust your reasoning and decide to investigate the light, turn to page 61.

If you accept Ned's feeling that it's nothing, turn to page 42.

30

The lights go out. The computer is silent. The screen is dead. The mechanical creature is gone.

You walk across the room and click on a small light above the computer. On the console is an instruction card. It reads: To Access Maze Schedule 32, Crossover B, Depress Control, Enter Run, Enter Coordinates 32M/46D/EFB.

You want to activate the computer by following the instructions, but you wonder what will happen if you are caught at the controls. Where did the thing go? What was it? And what if the three men return?

*If you try to operate the computer,
turn to page 55.*

*If you hide behind the curtains in the
room and wait, turn to page 75.*

The duty officer dials a two-digit number on his desk phone and talks rapidly for several minutes with a superior. You watch, impatiently at first, and then with growing alarm as the officer's face grows somber. Finally he hangs up and turns to you. His voice is grave.

"I'm afraid we have orders from Washington to detain you here for a while. They've just received word that your brother is being held hostage by OWD—the Organization for World Domination. Apparently one of their members overheard you two talking about your mission on the plane. Why did you leave your brother alone?

"We think OWD's been looting oil for a long time," he continues, "but now that they have your brother, they're going to be more careful than ever. We'll never get the chance to prove anything against them."

"We'll try negotiating with them," the officer concludes. "But I can't promise anything. It doesn't look good."

He's right.

The End

"I'll wait for you, Ned. No hurry," you say.

You, too, are intrigued by the paintings. You stare at the intricate designs. After a while the patterns swirl in a blur of color and rhythm, and you begin to feel dizzy.

Ned turns to you and holds out a small bronze box inlaid with pieces of coral and jade.

"Look at this. I found it under that pile of prayer rugs. I don't know why, but I know it's magical," he says. The storekeeper's back is turned as he busies himself with a group of tourists interested in buying a water pipe. In the box is a spicy-smelling salve.

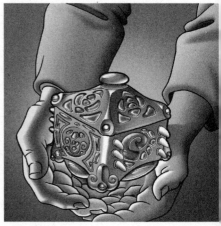

"Take some. Rub it on the back of your hand," Ned says.

His eyes are gleaming in a strange way. Suddenly he hands the box to you. As you watch, Ned rubs a large dollop of salve on his wrist and steps right into a mandala!

All that remains of him is a mocking laugh.

If you try to follow Ned, turn to page 58.

If you try to get out of the store, turn to page 84.

"Boris, we are friends," says Ned.

"I'm sorry. You must be mistaken. There is no Boris here," the man replies, but you can see a glimpse of something in his eyes. You're unsure about whether to press him or not; then you decide you'd better leave.

"Well, thanks anyway. Sorry to . . ." But you're interrupted by Ned. He's sort of half-singing and humming to himself.

"Here we go round the thornberry bush, the thornberry bush, the thornberry bush . . ."

The man leaning in the window stiffens slightly. You can see his eyes darken. His voice, which had been cold before, is frigid now. "Step out here a minute. Both of you."

Turn to page 36.

34

The three men take your silence as "yes." They stand and usher you out and back through the *medina*. You always carry a piece of red crayon in your pocket. It's been useful before in leaving a trail. You fish it out as carefully as you can, and as you follow, you mark the walls with the crayon at short intervals. The marks are small but easy to see if you look carefully.

As the men watch, you turn a corner. Minutes later, you return. The doorway is empty; the men have gone. You follow the crayon marks through the narrow passageway to the green staircase. Your heart is racing. Just as you are about to climb the stairs, the upstairs door opens. You flatten yourself against the wall in the shadow of the stairs. Maybe they won't see you!

The three men come down the stairs talking in low voices. Shivers of fear dart through your body. Quickly the men disappear down the passageway.

You are safe—at least for now. But should you follow the men, or search the room upstairs for clues to who they are?

If you follow the men, turn to page 109.

If you search the room, turn to page 26.

36

The man takes you to a spot a little ways from the taxi.

"Okay, you two. I think I know who you are. This is no game for amateurs. Get out of here before you get us all killed, and tell that incompetent director of yours to . . ."

"First of all, Boris, Thornberry isn't incompetent. She recruited you, didn't she?" Ned asks.

Boris blanches at your statement.

"Shhh! The desert has eyes, and ears. Leave now. I'll contact you at your hotel in Riyadh. Where are you staying?"

You tell him. He shouts at you in a harsh tone, commanding you to leave, for the benefit of anyone around. You and Ned drive off. Good to his word, Boris appears at your hotel.

"Here are the names of all the OWD agents worldwide. Take it back to Thornberry. Guard it with your lives. The key here is Hugo. You'll find him in London. Here's his address. That's all I can do for now. My life is in danger."

The list is delivered to Ms. Thornberry, and the CIA rounds up Hugo and the OWD gang, who were siphoning off oil from active wells to empty wells and old storage tanks. They are a desperate gang. But for now, the oil crisis is over.

The End

You crumple up the e-mail and throw it in an arching curve at the ornate wastebasket in a corner. It misses the wastebasket and falls to the floor.

"We're on our own, Neddie, old boy. We don't work for her anymore. We work for ourselves. I say we stay. Okay?"

"Sure. I'm with you," Ned says.

For days you and Ned search the arid desert of Egypt looking for clues. But this is one of the times Ned's special knowledge doesn't work. Your search appears fruitless. Meanwhile, the world oil crisis is getting worse.

One night, over dinner near the oil fields, you look at Ned and suggest, "Let's start over. This place is a dead end. We should have done more research on the whole thing. Let's go into town, check into a hotel, get a good night's rest, and start again."

The End

The next morning you, Ned, and Agent Ditwiller climb out of a long-range, high-speed courier jet in Casablanca, Morocco. Sunlight glares off the white concrete taxi apron, and you're glad you're wearing dark glasses.

Ditwiller stretches as he steps off the plane.

"So here we are. Now, O Great Wonder-kid, lead us on to Boris," he says to Ned in his most sarcastic tone.

"Hold your horses, great super agent," answers Ned placidly. "Boris will come to us."

But before you can make your next move, the back door of a service truck swings open. Three men dressed in burnooses open fire with machine guns.

For you, Ned, and Agent Ditwiller, Boris and the oil crisis are no longer problems. The agents from OWD calmly stow their weapons, close the door to the service truck, and drive away as if nothing had happened.

The End

40

"Ned, we've got to go to the island," you say. "We can't wait for your mysterious messages this time. I can feel it in my bones. I know I'm right."

Ned begins to stammer a refusal to follow your intuition, but Ms. Thornberry interrupts.

"I vote for the island, too. And my vote counts more than either of yours. Let's go."

Turn to page 46.

"Ms. Thornberry, Ned and I would like to examine the nuclear-waste disposal system first," you announce.

She hesitates for a moment.

"That's a hot issue, you know. Money, power, and reputation are tied up with that one."

You nod. "All the same, Ms. Thornberry, that's where we want to start."

Ms. Thornberry pulls down a large map of the world. It covers one entire wall of her office. She points to a spot on the map.

"Right here," she says. "The country of Hegeria has set aside this spot for the disposal of the nuclear waste of eleven nations."

"Ms. Thornberry," you ask, "do you have a detailed physical map of that spot?"

"Of course," she says. The second map is transparent and has raised relief. With the two maps combined, suddenly you can see all the physical dimensions of the Earth.

"Excellent idea," Ned says to you.

"Thanks," you say, but you're not sure what your idea was. (You're not going to tell Ned that, though.)

Turn to page 44.

42

"Okay, Ned, I suppose you're right. But I'm sure the light signals are for us."

Several hours later, you come to a stop at the gates of the Western Petroleum Group's main drilling and pumping office. You know they're a suspect group. This could be a front for the OWD field headquarters.

A man in a khaki uniform holding an automatic rifle stands by the gate. Behind him are six more armed, uniformed men. You hear the snick-snap of guns being loaded.

"State your business. Show your pass." His accent makes his English hard to understand.

He does not smile.

If you pretend you are lost, turn to page 77.

If you try to bluff your way in by saying "Boris sent us" and giving him your school cafeteria pass, turn to page 100.

Ned jumps up and points to the same spot Ms. Thornberry showed you. "There's a massive fault zone here. I read about it recently. It's even bigger than the San Andreas fault in California. And they're pumping all the waste right into it. I bet it's also interfering with the underlying strata of the oil fields. We've got to go there!"

A few hours later, equipped with the latest miniaturized Geiger counters and seismic measuring devices, you and Ned jet off to the independent nation of Hegeria. There you demand an immediate interview with the Minister of the Interior.

Go on to the next page.

You are met by a minor official outside the minister's office.

"I am sorry, but the Minister of the Interior is very, very busy. He has no time in his schedule for you." The aide turns away as though this dismissal is final. But you and Ned have come too far to give up so easily.

"Just one minute, please," you say firmly. "Tell him that unless he sees us immediately, we'll take this matter up with the World Organizing Committee—and they're tough, very tough. Here are our credentials." You show him an official letter of introduction from Ms. Thornberry. You also hope the aide doesn't realize you've invented the World Organizing Committee.

The aide looks at you, hesitates, but, not wanting to appear ignorant or get in trouble, points to a massive mahogany door. You push it open and enter.

Turn to page 49.

46

Two days later, the three of you and Helmut Saragura are aboard an aging twin-engine Grumman Goose. You are accompanied by two frogmen and two mountain rescue experts.

You chose the plane because it looks harmless, just an old island-hopper carrying fruits and vegetables and medical supplies from one island to another. Nobody would suspect it of being a mini-invasion force.

"There. Over there, about twenty degrees to the north. See it?" Saragura says.

You nod and peer out the window at a swirl of clouds rising like a mirage on a clear blue-green ocean.

Saragura continues to talk. "That's the island. Popped up like an asparagus. Volcano, you know. Happened ten years back. Covered with clouds all the time. The volcano smokes like crazy."

Turn to page 50.

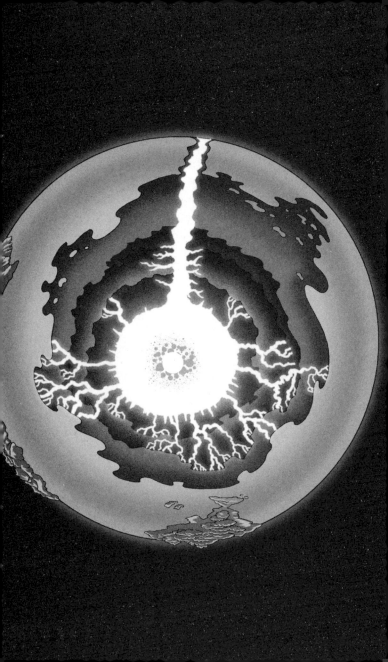

The Minister of the Interior is slumped behind his desk, his head in his hands and his shoulders dropping. Piles of paper litter the desk and the floor.

He looks up, surprised. "Who are you? Why are you here?"

"How can we help?" you answer.

"No one can," he replies. "The isotopes we pumped into the fault are loose now. They're following cracks deep into the Earth's crust like a giant underground river of death. The world is doomed! It's too late. Good day to you both. Leave now," he finishes abruptly.

You can see that you're not going to get too far with him today. Discouraged, you and Ned leave, returning to your hotel to wait a few days before approaching him again.

Turn to page 53.

50

The plane banks and makes a long, slow approach to a circular bay protected from ocean swells by a reef. The pontoons touch down on the calm water. Then you taxi to the rough shoreline and drop anchor.

"Okay. Time for action," announces Ms. Thornberry. "We'll split into two groups. One group will head for the volcano and circle it, looking for the nuclear plant. The other group will reconnoiter the shoreline by rubber raft and scuba gear." Ms. Thornberry looks at you. "I'm leading the island search team," she says.

If you decide to join the search for the nuclear plant, turn to page 64.

If you choose the frogman operation, turn to page 72.

"Let's go, Ned. Thornberry knows what's up.

"This was beyond us anyway," you say reluctantly.

Ned tries to argue, but you insist. The next afternoon, the two of you are on a commercial flight back to Washington, D.C. When you get to Ms. Thornberry's office, she seems nervous, almost terrified. You know she knows what's going on, but for some reason she is silent, powerless to act. *Who got to her, and why?* you wonder. But she's not telling you anything.

"I'm ordering you to stop the search right now. Boris is dead, and next it will be you two. I'll handle it," she says.

That night, the evening news announces that some of the oil fields are mysteriously active again. But production is very low. The price of a barrel of oil is now $1,000 and rising.

Ned nods slowly.

"I should have known it from the start. It was all a scam—a plot to drive up the price of oil. I bet Thornberry's in on it. Maybe she wasn't at the beginning, but she sure is now."

"Okay, Ned. Okay! But our hands are tied. What can we do?" you ask.

"Give me time. We'll think of something."

"You better think of something quick, because if they suspect we've found out . . ."

Before you finish your sentence, there's a knock at the door.

The End

You never get the chance. Two days later there is a deep, ominous rumble followed by the crackling sound of a major earthquake. Buildings waver, quiver, and tumble in upon themselves, as the Earth's crust heaves in a gigantic convulsion. The disappearing oil was only the smallest symptom of the world's fatal illness.

A cloud of poisonous air belches into the sky, eventually enveloping the Earth in a mist of death.

The End

54

You stand like an island in the stream of hurrying people. A dark doorway next to an open fruit stand catches your eye. What was that? One moment you think you see something; the next moment you aren't sure. It looked like a person motioning to you to come over, but sometimes your imagination plays tricks on you.

Nervously you look about for Ned and Patty. They are gone. When you turn around, you realize that there is a person in the doorway. He waves at you once again.

You approach the doorway cautiously. A man of about sixty is standing there. He is short, pudgy, and dark-skinned, and he's wearing a heavy wool vest over a white shirt and black trousers. He smiles at you.

"Come with me," he says.

"Who are you?" you ask.

"It is of little matter who I am. Who you are is important. Where the other two are is important. Come with me."

Turn to page 56.

You've always liked taking risks. You sit down at the computer, click the POWER ON button, and reread the instruction card describing the operation sequence. Lights flash on the screen. Rapidly the maze takes a new shape. This time the intricate lines create a three-dimensional map of the Earth.

What is this? You key in a REPEAT code, and yellow dots begin to appear on the map. They are concentrated in the oil-producing areas of the world!

You key in IDENTIFY PROGRAM and DISPLAY PROGRAM PURPOSE.

As you stare at the screen, the words ALPHA BASE appear in large, brilliant block letters. Beneath the words now appear the message: PROGRAM PURPOSE NOT AVAILABLE— ERROR IN SYNTAX.

What does that mean? ALPHA BASE? What is that? Why the ALPHA? Is there more than one base?

You hear noises outside the room. Now what? Startled, you click off the light and turn off the computer.

You think you see a door behind the half-closed curtains at one end of the room.

Should you try to make it to the door, or hide behind the curtains?

If you try to reach the door, turn to page 111.

If you hide behind the curtains,
turn to page 78.

56

That's too enticing to ignore. You take a deep breath and follow this man, who has already turned his back and has all but vanished into the doorway.

As you step into the darkness of a hallway, you see the glint of light on metal. Is it a knife, a gun, or just the man's wristwatch?

You don't have to go with him. You could back out. But what about your brother and Monsieur Patty?

If you go with the old man, turn to page 59.

If you return to the street to look for Ned and Monsieur Patty, turn to page 76.

You and Ned are ushered into a cube-shaped room, and your guards slam the door as they leave. The harsh overhead lights make you blink. Behind a metal desk sits a large man with a glistening bald head and clear blue eyes. He has folded his hands as if in prayer, but there is nothing kind about his look.

"So. Spies! That's it. You are American spies."

Ned looks up in surprise. Somehow he's figured it out again.

"Why, Boris, it's you, isn't it? You are Boris."

Fear flickers across the man's face. He raises his hand.

"Quiet, fools! Quiet! They'll hear you. Do you want us all to be killed?"

Boris—if it is Boris—opens a desk drawer, and then you see the blue-black glint of an automatic in his hand.

"You leave now!" he orders.

"But how can we? There are armed men out there," you say.

"That's your problem," answers Boris.

If you leave, turn to page 62.

If you try to negotiate with Boris, turn to page 96.

58

You rub the salve into your hand and step into the mandala. It's just like stepping through a doorway.

At first the world of the mandala seems like a giant sculpture garden filled with brightly colored metal geometric sculptures. They vibrate and shimmer in a way that hurts your eyes and throws you off balance. Finally you right yourself, just as your brother steps up to you from a circular structure that, only seconds before, appeared to be a long rectangular box.

Ned jabs you in the ribs. "I've got it all fixed. Let's get out of here," he says.

"What do you mean, Ned? What have you got all fixed? It looks like you fixed *us* just fine this time."

"One thing at a time. I found the oil. I fixed the leak. Follow me."

"How?" you ask.

"Same way we got in, stupid. Follow me."

Ned swims to a dot in space and vanishes.

If you follow him, turn to page 83.

If you stay put, turn to page 107.

"Lead the way, sir," you say. "Lead the way."

The old man smiles at you. "You will not be disappointed, I assure you," he tells you.

At any moment you expect to feel a gun in your ribs. But nothing happens, and you thread your way through a maze of dark passageways. Finally you reach a narrow green stairway. The old man points upward.

At the top of the steps is a door. The old man tells you to open it. You push against it, and it finally swings open on old rusted hinges.

You have to bend down to enter the room. It is lit by one small bulb. In the dim light you see three men sitting cross-legged on the floor. One turns to you.

"Please be seated."

Turn to page 74.

"I'm sorry, Ned," you say. "You're not always right. Those flashes are a message. They're coming in standard Morse code sequence. I read it as 'SOS, Boris.'"

You tap the driver on the shoulder and point in the direction of the pyramid. He pulls to a stop, skidding slightly in the sand and dust of the road.

Ned refuses to follow you, so you're on your own. Brushing past the guides, who insist they're the only ones who know the "secrets of the Pyramids," you begin to climb the rough blocks of stone hewn centuries ago.

A small, ragged child bars your way.

"I am to be your guide. Very good guide."

"No, I don't need one." You try to brush past her, but she persists.

"I am to be your guide. Everyone needs a guide. Especially you!"

The lights flash again. Then they stop.

If you agree to let the girl be your guide,
turn to page 101.

If you refuse, turn to page 66.

"Okay, we'll go! You don't leave us much choice."

The man Ned believes is Boris scribbles a note on a piece of pink paper.

"Here. Show the guards this. It's all you'll need." He turns away from you, but he doesn't put away his gun.

"Okay, Ned. Let's go," you say.

Your hearts pounding, you leave the room. The instant you're outside the door, the guards aim their guns at you.

"Here! Wait. Here's a note—a safe-conduct."

You hand the pink slip to the man who seems to be in charge. He looks at it and begins to laugh.

"Safe-conduct, you say? Surely! It is a safe-conduct, in a manner of speaking."

You keep on moving toward the gate and your truck, eyes straight ahead and arms at your sides, forcing yourself not to run. Laughter follows you all the way to the truck.

Turn to page 89.

The guard takes you to a building in the center of the compound. It is made of concrete blocks and festooned with antennas.

"Wait here." The guard enters a narrow doorway and leaves you outside. Behind you is the squad of armed men. Drops of sweat roll down your forehead and off your nose. Minutes pass.

Finally the guard returns. "You two. In here."

Turn to page 57.

"Okay, Ms. Thornberry, lead the way. I'm for the old *terra firma* myself," you say.

"Right. Me, too," adds Dr. Saragura. "The *firma* the *terra,* the better for me." The wizened nuclear scientist mumbles to himself as he fusses with his miniaturized, hypersensitive Geiger counter.

The ground is cooled lava. It is smooth as glass in some places, while in others it's rough, uneven, and sharp. You have to watch your step.

"Who is responsible for this nuclear setup here, Ms. Thornberry?" you ask.

"Hard to tell. It's a group of business associates, very, very wealthy people from all over the world. They're beyond the law on this hunk of rock. It's their own kingdom."

"But what do they do with the energy?"

"We think it has something to do with a new orbiting satellite. But that, my friend, is what we're here to find out."

You nod. These people must have massive resources to be able to build a nuclear power plant on such a remote island.

Toward noon your search party suddenly breaks through the clouds into clear, hot sunlight. High above you, perched on the side of the volcano, is an immense geodesic dome. Next to the dome is a helicopter pad with two large sky-crane helicopters and three small high-speed jet copters. Five armed men stand by the helicopters.

Turn to page 70.

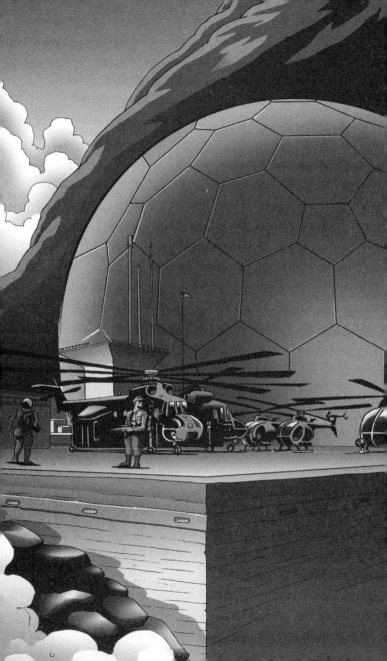

66

"I don't have time for you. Get out of my way!" you say angrily.

The child bows low, touching her hand to her forehead, to her breast, and then out to you in one smooth gesture. "Salaam! As you wish. You are making a mistake, I assure you. You need a guide," she says as she walks off.

At that moment a block of stone tumbles from above, knocking you over and crushing you. The light flashes again, but you never see it.

The End

You calculate your chances of getting to the rod: zero. Besides, you're intrigued by these creatures. You decide to play along.

"Okay, how can we help you?" you ask.

"You will see."

The fat man smiles and presses a button, releasing Ned from the frozen state. He rubs his arms and looks at you wonderingly.

"What happened?"

"It's okay, Ned," you answer. "Let me handle this."

Turn to page 71.

Suddenly you hear the truck starting off across the sand. You take a few steps after it, then stop. It's no use. You and Ned are alone.

There is nothing to do. No truck, no water, no food, no radio. You'll have to walk, and now even Ned has no idea where to go.

Toward nightfall the wind picks up. You both stumble on, but eventually you fall, exhausted. By dawn you and Ned are buried by a sand dune. The wind whistles a solitary note, and your tracks are covered.

The End

"Wow! Look at that!" you exclaim.

Ms. Thornberry grabs you by the shoulder and pulls you down.

"Shh!" she hisses. "Do you want those creeps to know we're here?"

Dr. Saragura is gibbering to himself and pointing at the Geiger counter, which is clicking away like popcorn popping at full blast. The dials have spun all the way to maximum.

"There's a meltdown at the plant! I know it. Those idiots built on the side of a volcano. It's huge, and it's melted down into the magma layer. It will keep going until it enters the Earth's core!"

"What's he talking about, Ms. Thornberry?" you ask.

She tries to calm the old man down, but he won't listen. Instead he runs madly up the steep slope toward the dome.

The guards haven't spotted him yet.

If you run after him, turn to page 104.

If you hide, thinking that it's impossible to catch him, turn to page 106.

The three green-suited beings step forward and motion you into the hatchway. It is an escalator going down into the ground beneath the shop. Underground, you enter a large, brightly lit room that looks almost like a subway station. Glowing signs on the wall read:

ZERMACROYD   OPPHOSS   ATLANTIS

Other green-suited men sit, waiting for the transporters, you assume.

You hear a ringing sound, and a sleep capsule slides into a bay next to the Zermacroyd sign. The three men, or whatever they are, point silently toward it. You have no real choice. In you go.

With an unimaginable speed you, Ned, and the three creatures shoot through the heavens, pass the Milky Way galaxy, and head into the quietness of pure space.

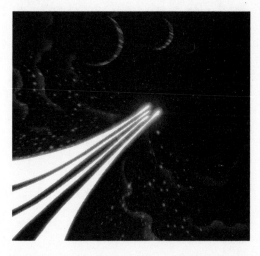

Turn to page 79.

72

Ned decides to join Ms. Thornberry and head toward the interior of the island and the nuclear plant. You think it best to split up, so you prepare yourself with a seven-pound weight belt, life vest, twin oxygen tanks, face mask, flippers, and a knife.

With the two frogmen in their black wet suits, you paddle off, passing the barrier reef through a small break. "Let's head for the south end of the island," you suggest. "We'll search the whole thing. Okay?" The two frogmen nod in agreement, and you're on your way.

In a few minutes you and the two frogmen are seventy-five feet down, checking the sandy bottom with a Geiger counter. From out of nowhere—or so it seems—four divers in bright red suits appear. They are armed.

The two frogmen are stunned by an electric pulse-prod. Then you're cornered near a spiny coral head. One red-clad diver holds you from behind while another cuts your air line. All your concern about missing oil, meltdowns, and CIA politics disappears in your desperate attempt to escape. You are frantic, and the end—your end— seems certain.

You don't make it.

The End

74

He does not smile, but you are not frightened.

You, too, sit on the floor and cross your legs. The old man vanishes through the door.

"What do you want?" you ask.

The man who spoke to you before answers, "We want you to give up this foolish search for the oil. It will only bring you trouble. Great trouble."

"What do you mean? You can't scare me."

"We mean you no harm. This is just a warning. Heed it. If not, well, danger lurks wherever you turn. Your brother Ned is being told the same thing. As for Monsieur Patty, he was a meddler from the start."

"You can go now. But give up the search."

Turn to page 34.

Sometimes it's best to play it safe. You decide to hide behind the curtains at one end of the room and wait to see what turns up.

You don't have to wait long. The door opens and in come three egg-shaped, orange-and-red beings about the size of softballs. They dart around the room in what seems to be a predetermined search pattern. They're making a clicking sound that reminds you of the sound of big, heavy June bugs banging against the walls of a lighted room in early summer. Then something speaks:

"Warning! Warning! Earth creature is present. Sound the alarm. Repeat. An Earth creature is present. Sound alarm. Give warning that security has been breached."

You're in for it now!

Turn to page 95.

76

The hairs on the back of your neck are standing straight up. You feel the tingling sensation you always connect with danger. It's a signal to get out—and fast.

You back into the street, babbling, "Oh, not right now. Something just came up. Gotta go. See you later!"

Just as you turn at the doorway, you are grabbed from behind. Strong arms encircle your neck, almost strangling you. "What's going on?" you gasp.

Those are your last words. That glint of metal was a knife. It's not glinting now, though. The bright finish is dulled with blood. Your blood.

Your body slumps to the rough cement floor. The dagger pins a note to your back. It reads:

LET THIS BE A WARNING! FORGET
THE OIL! WE ARE TOO POWERFUL
FOR ALL OF YOU.
—OWD

No one knows who signed the note.

The End

"We're sorry. We must have taken a wrong turn. Can you direct us?"

The man levels his rifle and points it at the two of you.

"No! You did not make any wrong turn. There are no turns. This is a very straight road, and it leads only here or to the desert." He motions with his rifle to the endless sands that surround you.

"So now you will come with me. Hands up. No camel business."

You protest. "Hey, what are you doing? We didn't do anything. We have rights, you know."

The man smiles grimly and keeps on going.

"Your rights have been removed. March!"

Turn to page 63.

Quickly you move behind the curtains and hold your breath. Moments later, the room is filled with the buzzing mechanical hum of a myriad of small egg-shaped orange and red creatures. They swarm around the computer in intricate, rapidly changing patterns—almost like a three-dimensional kaleidoscope.

You can't resist looking closer to see what they're doing. Just as you part the curtains, you hear a stentorian voice.

"Insert all laser straws!"

What in the world is a laser straw?

You don't have to wait long to find out. On the computer screen, the three-dimensional map of the Earth is rotating slowly. The other planets in the solar system appear on the screen as well. And in a far corner of the screen, you see a planet you don't recognize.

Turn to page 81.

At last the capsule comes to rest on what appears to be a large planet. A Hovercraft flies up, and the three aliens motion you inside it. You are taken to a large, light blue building. At least it looks blue, but it seems a color you've never seen before as though it's off the light spectrum you know on Earth. Inside the building you are led into an immense room paneled with what looks like wood.

There is a very solemn feel to the place. "It looks like a court," Ned whispers to you.

"I think it is," you reply.

Turn to page 93.

Lines begin to beam out of this new planet. As you watch, incredulous, they cross the screen, moving relentlessly toward Earth. Finally they pierce the Earth's surface in every oil field.

Now you understand. The lines are laser straws. They're being inserted into Earth's oil fields. The oil is being siphoned off and carried to another planet, a planet ruled by these misshapen ping-pong balls.

You dash from behind the curtains and lunge at the computer, trying desperately to reach the power button. Just as you hit it, turning the power off, you are hit by a paralyzing current coming from the crowd of colored globes.

You're finished.

The End

"We should head back, Ned," you say. "These people mean business."

Ned agrees reluctantly. He's a glutton for punishment, but occasionally you can reason with him. You drive back to Cairo and check into the hotel.

Outside the hotel you notice two men who look like Europeans. You are being watched—by OWD?

But you don't want to find out. You check into the hotel. The rooms are comfortable, and the two of you try to relax and make some sense out of what is going on. Suddenly there's a knock at the door. You hesitate before opening it, not sure what you might face. Then you screw up your courage.

It's a bellhop carrying an envelope on a silver plate. You rip it open. It's an e-mail sent to the hotel. You read:

RETURN U.S. IMMEDIATELY. PROBLEM
BEYOND YOUR REACH. DO NOT
CONTACT ME BEFORE RETURNING.
—THORNBERRY

"That's strange," you say. "Why didn't she e-mail us directly? How do we know it's from her?"

"She probably tried but we were out in the desert and your phone wasn't working out there," Ned replies.

Should you obey? Maybe Ms. Thornberry didn't send the e-mail. Maybe the same people who killed Boris did, just to get you out of the way.

If you obey the e-mail, turn to page 52.

If you ignore it, turn to page 37.

"Hold on, Ned! I'm coming."

The dot in space remains the same size until you reach it, and then *WHOOSH* it expands to a huge size.

You rush through the opening. Suddenly, without knowing how you got there, you're standing in the small store, staring at the mandala paintings. The container of salve is in your hand. Ned greets you with open arms.

"We did it! We did it!" he shouts, hugging you. The storekeeper turns and stares at you. He shakes his head and mumbles, "Crazy tourists."

"What have we done, Ned? Just what have we done? Besides taking a crazy trip in some Disneyland setup. How'd you do that, anyway?"

Ned doesn't answer. He takes the mandala from the wall and starts to negotiate a price with the storekeeper.

"Time to go. I've got it," he says at last. He walks out into the sunlit afternoon, and you follow.

Turn to page 86.

84

You rush to the entrance of the tiny shop, but the door is locked. You dart to the rear of the shop, knocking over a large Arabic screen.

Behind the screen is an old man. He is grotesquely fat, with a straggly white beard. Next to him is a machine with electronic gadgets.

A beam of light from the machine is focused on Ned, who is tied to a chair—gagged.

Turn to page 92.

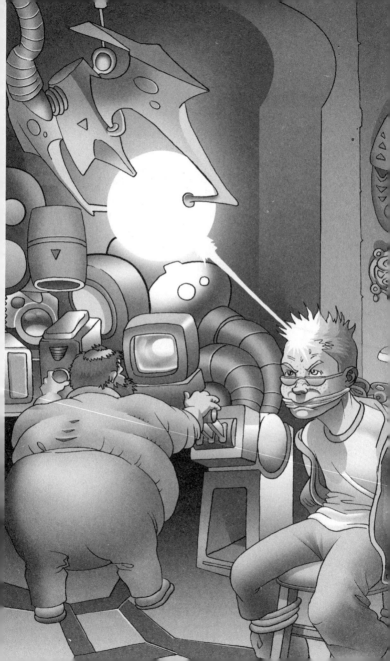

86

Getting a taxi in this crowded part of town is hard, but Ned does it. He tells the driver to go out into the desert. Once there, he leaves the cab and walks out onto the sand with you following. Finally Ned places the mandala on the sand, sits down before it, and begins one of his strange chants.

You can just make out what he's saying. It's an old Indian rain dance chant, but this time Ned's praying for oil.

Suddenly the mandala begins to move. It bursts into a glittering splash of gold, and from its center streams a flood of black liquid.

It's oil!

Oil pours from the mandala, and the sand swallows it as fast as it flows.

"Ned, what's going on?" you ask.

"It's simple," Ned answers. "Earth was using up its oil. So I just used the mandala to get back to a time before the oil started to run out. Then I brought it back to the present. You might call it a time pipeline."

"But but how did you figure all this out?" you sputter.

Ned just smiles.

Well, no one will believe this one, but at least the oil is back.

The End

"What do they want?" you ask.

"Power, domination. Oil is a key to power. Money, energy, military strength. They have the money; now they are adding the energy. Next will be the military."

"What can we do, Patty?" you ask.

Patty is already on the telephone, calling Interpol headquarters in Paris. After a few minutes of excited conversation, he hangs up and turns back to you.

"That was a good tip, my friend. Headquarters is on to them. We'll round them up. They've been quiet for some time. It had to be big; it certainly is. We appreciate your help. Leave the rest to us."

Ned is still asleep. Some help he was in this case. But you're sure he'll try to grab all the credit when he wakes up.

The End

"What's all this about our energy? Who are you?" you ask.

The fat man answers in a calm, pleasant voice.

"Your brother is correct. We are from the planet Zermacroyd. Yes, we are running out of energy, the energy that sustains our life force. The solar energy buried in your planet—oil—is like a fountain of youth to us."

"How . . . how do you get it?" you stammer.

"It's quite simple. We just change the oil from a liquid to a gas, compress it, and pump it through an optical hose."

He leans forward, and his voice suddenly becomes less pleasant. "Of course, we do have another source of energy available to us. We can merely drain it from Earthling bodies. But don't you agree that taking your oil is a more enjoyable solution?"

As he talks, the fat man rests the glass rod on the table next to Ned. You might be able to reach it and use it against him. The three green-suited humanoids have gathered together in the corner, probably waiting for commands from the fat man. Should you grab the glass rod and try to use it to escape? Or should you just offer to help the fat man? It might be your only way of helping Ned.

If you grab the glass rod, turn to page 91.

If you offer your help, turn to page 67.

At last you make it to the truck. The driver starts the engine, and at that moment a self-propelled rocket grenade whooshes through the air. It misses the truck and explodes in the desert with a roar.

"Hit it!" you yell. Two SUVs are already following you.

The driver slams the truck in gear and heads for the open desert. Somehow—neither of you knows how—you manage to outdrive the SUVs.

Turn to the next page.

90

One of them gets stuck in some sand, and the other falls farther and farther behind.

"We did it! We did it!" you yell, slapping Ned on the back.

"For now, yes. But OWD never sleeps. We haven't proven a thing yet. Are we going back there tomorrow?"

You stare at the shifting sands and wonder if you'll have the courage.

The End

You grab the rod. The fat man hurls himself at you, and the two of you fall to the floor together in a tangle of arms and legs. The rod slips from your grasp, and you desperately try to regain control of it.

"The rod! Get the rod!" the fat man shouts at the three creatures in the green suits. They throw themselves on top of you.

With a desperate lunge you grab the rod again and snap it in half. The moment it snaps the Zermacroyd creatures seem to wilt before your eyes. They lie limp and lifeless in a heap on the floor.

"You will . . . kill us. We . . . we . . . ne-ee-d. . ." whispers the fat man.

Then he collapses and is silent.

You know the world's oil flow will return to normal, but you wonder just how long it will take before Earth has to start looking elsewhere for its "fountain of youth."

The End

92

The fat man is holding a short glass rod that is connected to the mysterious machine. He waves the rod at the floor and suddenly the floor rolls back, revealing a glass-covered hatchway.

The hatchway looks especially incongruous in such an old building. It opens noiselessly, and a faint whine penetrates the air. Three figures wearing bright green skin-tight suits and clear plastic helmets emerge from the hatchway. They glide along as if on skates.

The fat man unties Ned's gag. Ned gasps and shouts, "They want our energy. They're from the planet Zermacroyd. He told me all about them. Don't give . . ."

The fat man waves the rod and Ned freezes, a look of horror on his face.

The fat man speaks. "Let us be reasonable, my young friend. Ned is upset. That is only natural. He will be quite all right. We haven't hurt him."

Turn to page 88.

Three fat men looking very much like the one you left back on Earth are sitting behind a large raised platform.

They start questioning you.

"What do you Earthlings do with your oil?" is the first question. A middle-aged man rises and advances to the front of the room. He is dressed in an orange suit without zippers or buttons.

"I object humbly, your honors. These two Earthlings have not been read their rights, nor have they been sworn in."

"Quite right. Well, let's get on with it, then."

Another man, who seems to be a clerk, rises and solemnly recites: "All creatures of the universe have a right to a fair trial. You are charged as representatives of the planet Earth with the crime of squandering natural resources, polluting, indifference to others in need in the multi-galaxy, and insensitivity to the future. These three citizens will judge you."

Turn to the next page.

The trial begins, and the questions are endless. How much oil does Earth use in a day? For what purposes? What is done about the air? What is done about the land? Is the oil shared equally throughout Earth?

You try to respond as best you can, but you're too stunned and exhausted to be convincing, even if you knew all the answers. You can tell the trial is going poorly. The judges confer in private for almost an hour. Then they return and read the verdict.

"This court finds Earth guilty of neglect toward itself and others. The punishment is to have all of Earth's oil resources removed and redistributed to other needy planets, forcing Earthlings to devise other and, we hope, better ways to solve their energy needs."

"You two will be held as hostages until we are satisfied that Earth has changed. You will not be harmed. You will be given the opportunity to live, work, and learn here on our planet."

"So be it."

The End

The clicking sound gets closer to the curtain. What should you do?

In the nick of time an inspiration hits you. You drop to your hands and knees on the floor and crawl out from behind the curtain barking like a dog!

You're not sure who's more surprised, you or the creatures. But you keep barking.

Then you hear the creatures muttering about someone leaving the door open and letting in this "pet sub-creature." Your trick worked! You are ushered downstairs and out into the alley. "Get out, you pest, and don't come back," says one of the creatures.

You hurry down the alley. You've got to find Ned and Patty and bring them back to the computer room.

But when, eventually, you do find them at the hotel and return, all you find is an empty room.

The End

You have to stall for time. Maybe you can convince Boris to help you.

"But Boris, I mean, if that's your name, we're from Thornberry," you say.

The mention of her name stops Boris cold. He blinks as if the bright afternoon sun were hitting him in the eyes.

"Thornberry. She sent you here? She did that?"

"Not exactly. It's Ned here. He brought us here, with her help. She didn't know exactly where you were."

He nods several times.

"So it begins. The end is near. First you come, then there will be others. I always knew it would happen."

"Don't worry, Boris. We're here to help," you say.

"Help? How can you two help me? I'm a marked man once it's known I'm a spy."

Go on to the next page.

"Ned! Come on, Ned," you say. "You got us into this, and you're putting Boris in a tough spot, too. What should we do?"

Ned walks over to the windowless wall and stares at a spiderweb.

"Boris, pretend we are your prisoners. Take us at gunpoint to the trucks. Then drive out north, a compass reading of thirty degrees for eleven kilometers. Someone will meet us. Don't ask how I know. I just do!"

"I guess I have no choice," Boris says gloomily. "With you here, my cover is blown unless I kill you. I'll go. Just get me to the U.S."

Turn to the next page.

Ned's plan works. His directions take you to a spot where a camel caravan is camping. Disguised as camel drivers, the three of you cross the Sahara and escape.

Was it just chance? Perhaps so, but you never can tell.

During the escape, Boris explains OWD's plot to "steal" the world's oil.

"You see, it's never actually being stolen. They have agents at each site. Gauges are altered, pumps are reversed, figures are manipulated until all the oil fields have reported huge drops in oil levels. OWD controls the information. Child's play, really."

"But why, Boris? Why?" you ask.

"Simple. Fear and greed are the biggest enemies of reason. With the world in a state of panic, OWD could take over. But I have their names, all the names."

Later, back in Washington, Ms. Thornberry receives a Congressional medal for conducting the successful investigation. She never mentions you and Ned.

Boris spends the rest of his life running a gas station in southern California.

The End

"Here's my pass. See for yourself. It was issued by headquarters. Let us through!" And you hold out your cafeteria pass.

The guard reaches for it. He holds it up, looks at it, squinches up his eyes, and turns the card around. Then you realize that he can't read. He's holding the card upside down!

"Come with me," he grunts.

You are marched off to meet a hulking, scowling man who yells, "What do you want?"

Ned gets the strange look in his eyes—the look of the secret knowledge.

Turn to page 33.

You hesitate for just a moment. Something the child said strikes a chord in your memory.

"Everyone needs a guide. Everyone needs a guide."

You turn to her. "Okay, lead the way. How much?"

The child smiles at you.

"Do not worry. Do not worry. Come my way."

The two of you climb the giant blocks under the hot Egyptian sun. Minutes later you are on the spot where you thought you saw the light. There is nothing there.

Then you see it . . .

Turn to the next page.

Drops of blood sparkle in the sun like rubies from a broken necklace. They are not dry yet. The fresh blood forms a trail down one side of the pyramid. You follow.

At the base of the pyramid is the crumpled form of a huge man. He is obviously dead. A note is pinned to his shirt—written in English!

> THIS WAS BORIS. IF YOU DON'T TURN
> BACK, THIS WILL BE YOU!
> —OWD

You look up. Your guide has disappeared. The hot wind of the desert sweeps over you, but you are chilled to the bone.

Turn to page 112.

There's probably no time to lose. Whoever assassinated this man is in dead earnest.

Ned tells the driver to leave the road and head across the desert. The driver reluctantly agrees. You can tell he doesn't trust you.

You head out into the trackless waste of sand, where Ned directs the driver to a series of large dunes. Several times the balloon tires of the truck bog down in the sand, but each time the three of you manage to dig the truck out and continue.

"Ned, where are we going?" you demand.

"Just wait, you'll see," is all he'll say.

Sure enough, later that afternoon you come across an abandoned campsite. You get out of the truck and head across the sweeping sands to investigate. You find two six-man tents; several large drums, which must once have held water; and a pile of empty cartons, which once contained food. Among the trash you also discover a crumpled map marking the oil wells in the region. At the bottom of the map is a date—today!

Turn to page 69.

"I'll get him," you say. "You stay here, Ms. Thornberry."

"Don't be a fool. The guards will get you. These people mean business."

You ignore her and run after Saragura, who has suddenly stopped in his tracks. He is screaming at the top of his lungs and suddenly the words start making sense to you.

"The volcano! It's going up!"

You look up at the cone just as it erupts in a brilliant flash of red, orange, white, and black. The sky is filled with the searing heat of the explosion.

You take one last breath before you and the island are incinerated.

The End

Good decision! It was a tough one to make; you've come to like Saragura, but seconds later one of the guards spots the old man in his dash to the dome. There is a short blast from an automatic weapon, and the scientist drops in his tracks.

You, Ned, and Ms. Thornberry duck back into the safety of the cloud cover. You're in a state of shock having seen Saragura go down.

"Oh no, what do we do now?" you ask.

"Let's head back for the plane. We don't have much time. That Geiger counter was so hot, we'd better get off this island as fast as possible."

"Okay. Let's go."

Right behind you, the guards are shouting to each other and fanning out in the cloud-fog, trying to find you. They must have picked up your presence with sensing devices.

Finally you make it to the cove. The plane is gone!

You gasp. "Looks like this is it for us. We'll never get off this island alive."

Ms. Thornberry nods in agreement. The three of you sit, staring out to sea, on the rough lava at the edge of the water. You can hear the searchers coming closer and closer.

Turn to page 108.

"I'm tired of taking your orders," you shout after the departing Ned.

You walk around in the mandala. After a while your anger toward Ned lessens, and you wonder what he meant by "getting it all fixed." You decide to go and find out, but you can't. You're trapped where you are.

Ned knew how to get out, but you don't. Each time you try to exit the way he did, *bang!*—you end up being pushed back by an invisible force.

Maybe it isn't so bad where you are after all. You decide to relax and enjoy it. Ned and the oil and the real world—whatever that was—are pretty dim memories anyway. Let them take care of themselves.

The End

You might as well try to make some sense of all this before you're caught. "Ms. Thornberry, why was that reactor built here anyway? Who built it?"

"This group—they call themselves the International Energy Corporation—says they're building a nuclear power plant here to provide energy for their worldwide enterprises. I think they're a cover for OWD," she answers.

"How do they get the energy off this island?" you ask.

"They say they're going to beam it up as microwave radiation to satellites of theirs, then send it down to receivers placed where they need it."

"Sounds like you don't believe them."

"The CIA believes that this group is really trying to produce plutonium and create its own nuclear bomb."

"Why?"

"Obvious: They want to hold the world ransom. It's not surprising, really. They just didn't count on a meltdown."

You nod and ask one final question before you are captured. "What about the oil? Who took it? Where did it go?"

Ms. Thornberry looks pensive for a minute, and then says simply, "Used up, I guess. Odd how it happened like that all at once. We'd been warned for years, but we never listened."

Out of the fog come three men. You are doomed.

The End

You can always come back to the room upstairs. It would be wiser to follow these men now.

They blend into the crowd so well that it's hard to keep an eye on them. Often you can only tell who you are following because they move together as a group.

The crowd thickens, and it is even harder to keep up with them. Then you realize that they have headed into a giant, open-air market. Wherever you look, you see wall-to-wall people, and in an instant the three men disappear. There is no sign of them anywhere.

A man lugging a large wicker basket of fruit bumps into you, almost knocking you down. You shake your head. You're furious at yourself for losing them.

You'll need reinforcements to search the market. Angry and disheartened, you make your way back to the hotel. Ned and Monsieur Patty don't show up until late that evening, and neither one will say where he's been. Patty looks glum. Ned makes a face and repeats, "It was too late. Too late." He falls into a deep sleep before you can find out any more from him.

Briefly you tell Patty what happened to you that afternoon. The more you tell him, the more interested he becomes.

Turn to page 113.

You make it to the door behind the curtains. It opens into a room filled with more of the glowing mechanical creatures like the one you surprised earlier. They seem inactive, stacked like so many eggs waiting to be delivered to a supermarket.

This is not for you!

Spinning around, you dash out a half-open door in the far wall. It opens onto empty air. You fall three floors, but your life is saved when you land in a wagonload of melons.

Hours later, after you've paid the irate fruit vendor, the police release you. But when you return to the scene of the action, bringing an incredulous police lieutenant with you, all evidence of strange creatures and computers is gone!

You have had enough of this business. Now it's time to search for Ned. You're sure he can manage on his own, but you might as well help him out. After all, he is your brother.

The End

112

Below you are the road, the driver, and Ned.

Boris's body is already stiffening. Cautiously you leave the spot, hoping you're not the assassins' next target. At last, you reach the car.

"Ned, it was Boris. He was killed," you say.

"How do you know it was Boris?"

"There was a note. The note said that the man—the body—was Boris."

"Do you believe everything you read?"

You don't answer.

"Well, let's get out of here," Ned says.

You're wondering, though, whether you should go back for help. This is beginning to seem like too much for you.

If you go back for help, turn to page 82.

If you continue on, following Ned's directions, turn to page 103.

Monsieur Patty stares at you, his dark eyes burning intently.

"Tell me more," he says. "Did these people say who they were?"

You stare back. Patty has some answering to do, too. You fire a question back at him.

"Before I tell you, just where did you take Ned? Where did you go?"

Patty grimaces. "We were duped. Led astray by some idiot who attracted Ned's attention. How do you say it? A wild duck chase?"

You nod. It's just the kind of trouble Ned would get into. You give Patty a detailed explanation of the room, the men, and their warning.

Patty nods. Then he says abruptly, almost shouting, "You must remember everything. Did they say who they were?"

As best you can remember, the three men said nothing about who they were. But suddenly you remember something.

"I think they said OWD would be angry if they failed. OWD. I don't know what it is. Do you, Patty?"

Patty stares at you. "OWD," he says in a half whisper. "OWD means Organization for World Domination. We infiltrated that group last year, but there was no clue to them being in on this oil business."

Turn to page 87.

ABOUT THE ARTISTS

Illustrator: Mariano Trod was born in Argentina in 1974. He studied art at the Fine Arts School "Juan Mantovani." Between 1998-2001 he worked as Art Director in the educational cartoon "Astronitos" for Astrokids S.A. Today he is the Art Director for Sismostudio.

Illustrator: Claudio Griglio was born in Argentina in 1976. He studied with the celebrated Argentinian comic artist Roberto Formento. Claudio was the Director of design at Rafaela City Hall between 2001-2005. Today he is the Coordinator of the illustration department at Sismostudio.

Illustrator: Andrés Rossi was born in Argentina in 1979. He has a Social Communications degree from the Santiago del Estero Catholic University. He was Junior Designer for Artegraf Design between 1995-1996. He was Junior Designer at the Design Office at Rafaela City Hall between 1996-1999. Between 1999-2002 he worked as Producer on the educational cartoon "Astronitos" for Astrokids S.A. Now he is the CEO of Sismostudio.

Cover Artist: Marco Cannella was born in Ascoli Piceno, Italy on September 29, 1972. Marco started his career in art as decorator and illustrator when he was a college student. He became a full-time professional in 2001 when he received the flag-prize for the "Palio della Quintana" (one of the most important Italian historical games). Since then, he has worked as illustrator for the Studio Inventario in Bologna. He has also worked as scenery designer for professional theater companies. He works for the production company ASP srl in Rome as character designer and set designer on the preproduction of a CG feature film. In 2004 he moved to Banglore, India to work full-time on this project as art director.

ABOUT THE AUTHOR

R. A. Montgomery attended Hopkins Grammar School, Williston-Northampton School and Williams College where he graduated in 1958. Montgomery was an adventurer all his life, climbing mountains in the Himalaya, skiing throughout Europe and scuba-diving wherever he could. His interests included education, macro-economics, geo-politics, mythology, history, mystery novels and music. He wrote his first interactive book, *Journey Under the Sea,* in 1976 and published it under the series name *The Adventures of You.* A few years later Bantam Books bought this book and gave Montgomery a contract for five more, to inaugurate their new children's publishing division. Bantam renamed the series *Choose Your Own Adventure* and a publishing phenomenon was born. The series has sold more than 260 million copies in over 40 languages.

For games, activities, and other fun stuff, or to write to Chooseco, visit us online at cyoa.com

The History of "Gamebooks"

Although the *Choose Your Own Adventure* series, first published in 1976, may be the best known example of interactive fiction, it was not the first.

In 1941, the legendary South American writer Jorge Luis Borges published *Examen de la obra de Herbert Quain* or *An Examination of the Work of Herbert Quain,* a short story that contained three parts and nine endings. He followed that with his better known work, *El jardín de senderos que se bifurcan,* or *The Garden of Forking Paths*, a novel about a writer lost in a garden maze that had multiple story lines and endings.

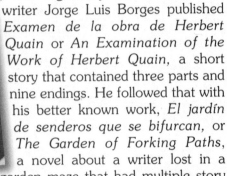

Jorge Luis Borges

More than 20 years later, in 1964, another famous South American writer, Julio Cortazar, published a novel called *Rayuela* or *Hopscotch*. This book was composed of 155 "chapters" and the reader could make their way through a number

Julio Cortazar

of different "novels" depending on choices they made. At the same time, French author Raymond Queneau wrote an interactive story entitled *Un conte à votre façon,* or *A Story As You Like It*.

Early in the 1970s, a popular series for children called *Trackers* was published in the UK that contained multiple choices and endings. In 1976,

Journey Under the Sea, 1st Edition

R. A. Montgomery wrote and published the first interactive book for young adults: *Journey Under the Sea* under the series name *The Adventures of You*. This was changed to *Choose Your Own Adventure* by Bantam Books when they published this and five others to launch the series in 1979. The success of CYOA spawned many imitators and the term "gamebooks" came into use to refer to any books that utilized the second person "you" to tell a story using multiple choices and endings.

Montgomery said in an interview in 2013: "This wasn't traditional literature. The *New York Times* children's book reviewer called *Choose Your Own Adventure* a literary movement. Indeed it was. The most important thing for me has always been to get kids reading. It's not the format, it's not even the writing. The reading happened because kids were in the driver's seat. They were the mountain climber, they were the doctor, they were the deep-sea explorer. They made choices, and so they read. There were people who expressed the feeling that nonlinear literature wasn't 'normal.' But interactive books have a long history, going back 70 years."

Young R. A. Montgomery

Choose Your Own Adventure Timeline

1977 – R. A. Montgomery writes *Journey Under the Sea* under the pen name Robert Mountain. It is published by Vermont Crossroads Press along with the title *Sugar Cane Island* under the series name *The Adventures of You*.

1979 – Montgomery brings his book series to New York where it is rejected by 14 publishers before being purchased by Bantam Books for the brand new children's division. The new series is re-named *Choose Your Own Adventure*.

1980 – *Space and Beyond* initial sales are slow until Bantam seeds libraries across the U. S. with 100,000 free copies.

1983 – CYOA sales reach ten million units of the first 14 titles.

1984 – For a six week period, 9 spots of the top 15 books on the Waldenbooks Children's Bestsellers list belong to CYOA. *Choose* dominates the list throughout the 1980s.

1989 – Ten years after its original publication, over 150 CYOA titles have been published.

1990 – R. A. Montgomery publishes the *TRIO* series with Bantam, a six-book

series that draws inspiration from future worlds in CYOA titles *Escape* and *Beyond Escape*.

1992 – ABC TV adapts Shannon Gilligan's CYOA title *The Case of the Silk King* as a made-for-TV movie. It is set in Thailand and stars Pat Morita, Soleil Moon Frye and Chad Allen.

1995 – A horror trend emerges in the children's book market, and Bantam launches *Choose Your Own Nightmare*, a series of shorter CYOA titles focused on creepy themes. The subseries is translated into several languages and converted to DVD and computer games.

1998 – Bantam licenses property from *Star Wars* to release *Choose Your Own Star Wars Adventures*. The 3-book series features traditional CYOA elements to place the reader in each of the existing *Star Wars* films and feature holograms on the covers.

2003 – With the series virtually out of print, the copyright licenses and the *Choose Your Own Adventure* trademark revert to R. A. Montgomery. He forms Chooseco LLC with Shannon Gilligan.

2005 – *Choose Your Own Adventure* is re-launched into the education market, with all new art and covers. Texts have been updated to reflect changes to technology and discoveries in archaeology and science.

2006 – Chooseco LLC, operating out of a renovated farmhouse in Waitsfield, Vermont, publishes the series for the North American retail market, shipping 900,000 copies in its first six months.

2008 – Chooseco publishes CYOA *The Golden Path*, a three volume epic for readers 10+, written by Anson Montgomery.

2008 – Poptropica and Chooseco partner to develop the first branded Poptropica island, "Nabooti Island" based on CYOA #4, *The Lost Jewels of Nabooti*.

2009 – *Choose Your Own Adventure* celebrates 30 years in print and releases two titles in partnership with WADA, the World Anti-Doping Agency, to emphasize fairness in sport.

2010 – Chooseco launches a new look for the classic books using special neon ink.

2011 – Reads of *Fabulous Terrible*, Chooseco's YA novel for girls, reach 1 million on Wattpad.com

2013 – Chooseco launches eBooks on Kindle and in the iBookstore with trackable maps and other bonus features. The project is briefly hung up when Apple has to rewrite its terms and conditions for publishers to create space for this innovative eBook type.

2014 – Brazil and Korea license publishing rights to the series. 20 foreign publishers currently distribute the series worldwide.

2014 – Beloved series founder R. A. Montgomery dies at age 78. He finishes his final book in the *Choose Your Own Adventure* series only weeks before.

2015 – Anson Montgomery's "lost title" original #185 *Escape from the Haunted Warehouse* receives glowing reviews from *People Magazine* and CBC Radio, and he is included with 24 other writers in the 2015 Twitter Fiction Festival.

THE ABOMINABLE SNOWMAN

CHOOSE FROM 28 ENDINGS!

BY R. A. MONTGOMERY

JOURNEY
UNDER THE SEA

CHOOSE FROM 42 ENDINGS

BY R. A. MONTGOMERY

SPACE AND BEYOND

CHOOSE FROM 44 ENDINGS!

BY R. A. MONTGOMERY

CHOOSE YOUR OWN ADVENTURE® 4

THE LOST JEWELS OF NABOOTI

CHOOSE FROM 38 ENDINGS!

BY R. A. MONTGOMERY

MYSTERY OF THE MAYA

CHOOSE FROM 39 ENDINGS!

BY R. A. MONTGOMERY

HOUSE OF DANGER

CHOOSE FROM 20 ENDINGS!

BY R. A. MONTGOMERY

RACE FOREVER

CHOOSE FROM 33 ENDINGS!

BY R. A. MONTGOMERY

ESCAPE

CHOOSE
FROM 27
ENDINGS

BY R. A. MONTGOMERY

LOST ON THE AMAZON

CHOOSE FROM 28 ENDINGS!

BY R. A. MONTGOMERY

PRISONER OF THE ANT PEOPLE

BY R. A. MONTGOMERY

TROUBLE ON PLANET EARTH

BY R. A. MONTGOMERY

WAR WITH THE EVIL POWER MASTER

CHOOSE FROM 28 ENDINGS!

BY R. A. MONTGOMERY

SECRET
OF THE NINJA

CHOOSE
FROM 29
ENDINGS

BY JAY LEIBOLD

ISLAND OF TIME

CHOOSE FROM 12 ENDINGS!

BY R. A. MONTGOMERY

THE TRAIL OF LOST TIME

BY R. A. MONTGOMERY

Trouble Trivia Quiz

Have you saved the Earth from destruction? Do you believe in your brother Ned's Extrasensory Perceptions? Can you solve this trivia quiz?

1) What important resource is missing at the start of your adventure?
A. Coal
B. Food
C. Oil
D. Bicycles

2) Who is Ned?
A. Your old friend from school.
B. Your brother.
C. You don't know him at all.
D. Your father.

3) You and Ned must decide between which two locations to start your search for the oil?
A. Cairo, Egypt and New York City
B. Reykjavik, Iceland and Santiago, Chile
C. Montpelier, Vermont and Montreal, Canada
D. Saudi Arabia and Washington, D.C.

4) What does OWD stand for?
A. Organization for World Domination.
B. Owls With Darkness.
C. Oil Without Digging.
D Organization for Winter Dispersement.

5) Where does Ms. Thornberry work?
A. The oil refinery in Saudi Arabia.
B. The Capitol building in Washington, D.C.
C. The local grocery store.
D. The CIA.

6) Who insists on being your guide?
A. Boris
B. Ned
C. A small, messy child.
D. Ms. Thornberry

7) Who do you find dead with a creepy note on his back?
A. Boris
B. Ned
C. Hank
D. No one

8) What does Ned find in the shop?
A. A magical box filled with salve.
B. A crystal ball.
C. A cookie.
D. A magic carpet.

9) Who does Ms. Thornberry send with you to search for Boris?
A. Dr. Saragura
B. A small child
C. Ditwiller
D. No one, you go it alone.

10) Where does Ned disappear?
A. The mandala shop.
B. Washington, D.C.
C. Thornberry's office.
D) The plane.

TROUBLE ON PLANET EARTH

This book is different from other books.

You and YOU ALONE are in charge of what happens in this story.

There are dangers, choices, adventures, and consequences. YOU must use all of your numerous talents and much of your enormous intelligence. The wrong decision could end in disaster—even death. But don't despair. At any time, YOU can go back and make another choice, alter the path of your story, and change its result.

The Earth's oil fields are drying up and the world is thrown into chaos. As you watch the news reports, your brother Ned has one of his premonitions: the Earth's oil is being stolen. But who would steal it? And how? Should you put your investigation skills to work in Saudi Arabia, another of Ned's "premonitions"? Or should you travel first to CIA Headquarters to see what they have to say?

Let's hope the Earth's fuel lasts long enough to let you find out!